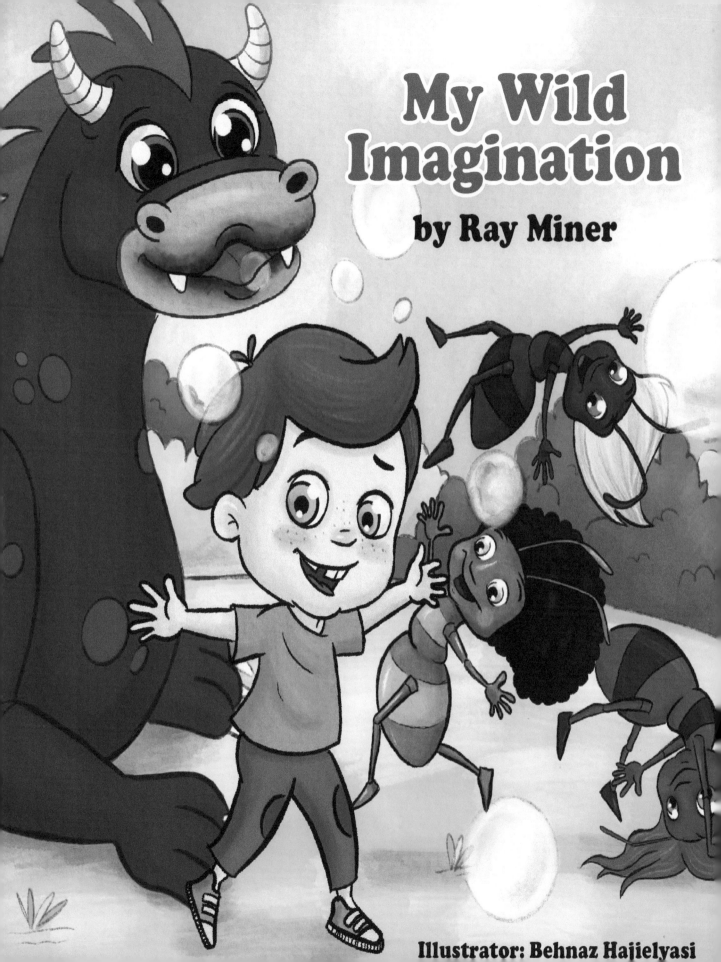

My Wild Imagination

by Ray Miner

Illustrator: Behnaz Hajielyasi

My Wild Imagination

Author: Ray Miner

Illustrator: Behnaz Hajielyasi

To Wyatt and Everett, two youngsters who
love a grand adventure

Zipping out the door one day I
stopped dead in my tracks

Before me on the walk there played a
group of hairy ants

Ants don't have hair, I said out loud, and neither do they play, but these were turning flip-flops as they went along their way

I left them to their antics as I raced around the house

Look out, I dodged, I'd almost ran into a dragon's mouth

His eyes were red, his mouth was black, scorched from fire, no doubt

I ran to get away from him before he could breathe out

He chased me, oh, he
caught me and I thought
that I was dead

But when he breathed
that awful breath

He blew bubbles out instead!

A dragon blowing bubbles?
Ridiculous I said

I turned to leave and bumped into

A lion being fed.

The lion looked up at me as he gnawed upon a bone.
I knew I was his next meal so I wheeled and raced
for home.

He chased me as I zig-zagged then
I heard an awful ROAR!

And as he lunged to catch me
I went zigzag through the door

My heart was beating faster, I just barely got away

Then from my room I heard strange sounds, like animals at play.

Creeping I went closer, what could cause such jubilation

And peeking
through the
door I saw

My wild
imagination!

About the author...

Ray Miner spent 30 years in education as a guidance counselor. Along the way, he wrote and recorded songs and wrote poems for his and his wife's two daughters. Some of his songs can be heard on youtube, including many from the "Old Dogs, New Tricks" cd. He has written several Christmas songs recorded by Briana Kay on the "It's Christmas" cd. After retiring, he decided to concentrate on turning the poetry into illustrated children's books. My Wild Imagination is the second of the poems to experience this metamorphosis, Bedtime having been the first.

About the illustrator...

Behnaz Hajielyasi was born in Iran. She has a Bachelor of Fine Arts degree and has been working as an illustrator and a graphic designer for more than 7 years. Also, Behnaz has published books on Amazon. She loves children and drawing for them. Her illustrations are based on digital painting, watercolor and color pencil techniques.

Behnaz.hajielyasi@gmail.com

Other works by Ray Miner

Bedtime   Children's picture book

Lemonade   Adult fiction short story, Amazon Kindle

It's Christmas, a Christmas cd featuring original Christmas songs, performed by Briana Kay, available on itunes, Amazon, and others

Other original songs, including **Old Dog, New Tricks** cd by Ray Miner available on itunes, Amazon, etc., and youtube

CPSIA information can be obtained
at www.ICGtesting.com
Printed in the USA
BVHW022142090921
616497BV00007B/116